Phenomena

Polly Scott

Published by Trellis Publishing, 2021.

This is a work of fiction. Similarities to real people, places, or events are entirely coincidental.

PHENOMENA

First edition. July 1, 2021.

Copyright © 2021 Polly Scott.

ISBN: 979-8224281169

Written by Polly Scott.

PHENOMENA

1

SHOUT AT THE DEVIL

JESSICA BARKLEY

Dust swirled in a shaft of light coming through the window. The building was old and faded. Letters on the sign she had passed outside had been bleached by the sun, leaving behind more of a whisper than a declaration: Living Waters Orphanage. Ruth walked quietly down the hall. Finger paintings on yellowed paper clung desperately to the walls. A bulletin board was pinned with pictures of smiling children with sad eyes. Their faces filled her with longing and despair. There were no more laughs here, no more children running down the hall. No more hopeful couples coming to take them home. The orphanage had been closed down for years, sitting here empty with no purpose. Ruth clutched her purse as she continued down the hall. The woman on the phone had said to follow the main entrance to the last door on the right.

Ruth's breath was quick and shallow. Her clothing was black, and her red hair was down around her shoulders. Ever since the incident, she had tried to make herself as inconspicuous as possible. Her long hair was like a wall, protecting her from the rest of the world. It had been hard to talk about it. She was afraid people wouldn't believe her. She needed somewhere to go where people wouldn't judge her or think she was insane. That's when she had seen the ad.

Her favorite coffee shop had a wall set aside for small businesses to advertise. Most of the flyers were for teenagers trying to get jobs mowing lawns or for lost pets in the area. She typically just let her eyes glance over them while she waited in line, not really taking in the words. Something about one of the flyers caught her attention. It had a cross in the middle with text above and below saying, "Survivor support group. Taking back possession of your life after possession." There was a number on the ad to call for more information. Ruth had memorized the number and called later that evening. The woman who answered sounded young and so full of life. She gave Ruth the address and time of the next meeting. Despite desperately wanting help, she still had to force herself to go. The closed down orphanage wasn't exactly a hopeful place to meet.

A sign on the last door on the right had the same flyer Ruth had seen at the coffee shop. Her hands trembled as she reached out for the silver handle on the door. She pushed the door open. The hinges groaned in protest. The room was about the size of a classroom, and there were five chairs arranged in a circle. Four of them were taken. A young blonde woman stood up as she entered, "Hi! You must be Ruth." She extended her hand as Ruth joined them, "I'm Lucy." Her smile looked out of place amidst the dust trailed floor and the grimy windows.

Ruth pried one hand off of her purse strap and shook Lucy's hand, "Nice to meet you." Her voice was timid as she took her seat. The stale air filled her lungs as she breathed in and out. She sat stiffly and looked around at the other members of the group.

"Why don't we go around and introduce ourselves?" Lucy seemed a little too happy for the circumstances. Her bubbly attitude contrasted darkly with the atmosphere of the room. She was like a buzzing neon sign fighting not be swallowed by the night fog. She sat back down and looked at the girl on her left.

"I'm Brandy. It's been two months since my possession." Brandy had dark hair and a small tattoo of a heart on her collarbone. Her sultry eyes peered at them from above her dark, red lips.

"I'm Heather. It's been a year since my possession." Heather was blonde. She wore a tiny gold cross around her neck. Where Lucy's personality was like a buzzing neon sign, Heather's was more delicate, like starlight.

"I'm Jackie. It's been about a month since my possession." Jackie had dark hair with purple streaks in it. Her nails were painted black. She gave Ruth a small, apathetic wave as she spoke. A smirk played across her face.

It was Ruth's turn now. All of their responses had seemed structured. She followed the pattern, "I'm Ruth. It's been two weeks since I was possessed." All of the other girls looked younger than she was. Were they teenagers? Maybe they were in their early twenties? She looked at the wrinkles on her knuckles. She was already in her thirties, and most of her time had been wasted frivolously.

"Good! Everyone is doing great. Who would like to share their story first?" Lucy's eyes sparkled with joy as she looked around the room, "You can tell us how you felt, anything you remember, how you are dealing with it now, and really just anything you feel comfortable sharing." Warmth beamed out of her as she talked.

There was a brief silence. All of the women were waiting to see who would speak first. "I'll go." Heather sat up straighter in her chair, "You would think having a year to process this would make it easier to talk about," she gave a small nervous laugh, "but it doesn't really. I was sixteen when I first became possessed. I don't know why I was chosen, but I think it may have been punishment for my father." Heather made eye contact with the other girls as she spoke. She was more somber now. "My dad performs exorcisms for the church. I think that possessing me was a demonic way to get back at him for years of undoing their work. I grew up around it all the time, but nothing can prepare you for when it happens to you." Heather swallowed before continuing, "I just get bits and pieces when I try to remember." She looked at the floor as if she were searching for answers, "I remember losing pieces of time. Like I would be eating breakfast, and the next time I looked down I was in my room getting ready for bed. Or I would be watching TV, and the next time I blinked I would be cooking dinner. Several times I would be driving, and then I would look up and be in a completely different part of town, as if my body were on autopilot. Everything was disconnected. Nothing is more frightening than not having control over your own body and not remembering how you got somewhere. It was the most terrifying experience I've ever had." She looked up at the group as the other girls nodded. "I still pray every night for protection and for help on overcoming all of this. When I saw your sign," Heather tilted her head towards Lucy, "I just felt like God wanted me to be here for some reason, so that's why I'm here."

"That was an excellent job at sharing!" Lucy smiled reassuringly. "Who would like to go next?"

"I guess I can go." Brandy flipped her hair behind her shoulder. "I was at work when I had my first demonic episode." She paused and cocked her head to the side, "Well at least it's the first one anyone told me about, showed me really."

"What do you mean showed you?" Jackie leaned in as she listened.

"Um, well, they caught it on tape."

"Like, what, a security camera?" Jackie squinted trying to understand.

Lucy straightened her shirt, "Why don't we practice active listening, and just let Brandy talk?" She raised her eyebrow at Jackie who leaned back in her chair and crossed her arms.

"It's ok," Brandy clasped her hands together as she continued. "I used to do adult films. During one of the scenes, I levitated and spouted off some strange language. At first they thought some of the set people were in on the joke, but there weren't any wires. There wasn't really any logical explanation for what happened. Now, no one wants to work with me. No one will hire me. No one who knows anyway. It pretty much ended my career. Honestly, I couldn't believe it was me when I saw the tape. I thought they were playing a joke on me, but the fear in their eyes was real." Brandy took a deep breath, "I called a priest to come talk with me. He said that he believed I was possessed. That's a hard thing to hear, but he helped me through it." Brandy's mouth formed a small smile as she remembered the priest fondly, "I've never really been a religious person, but if there can be something so awful in the world, then there has to be something good, too." Brandy looked up towards the ceiling, "There has to be."

Lucy followed Brandy's gaze then quickly said, "Well done, Brandy. Jackie? Why don't you tell us your story?"

"I didn't want an exorcism. I welcomed my demon." Jackie sat back up as she spoke. Heather leaned away from her as she continued, "He made me feel alive and powerful. All of you were weak. Too weak to truly enjoy it. I bet you didn't even touch yourself during it." She turned towards Brandy, "Did you know that possession leads to heightened sexual pleasure? My climaxes were so intense, it was amazing." Jackie writhed in her chair as she remembered.

"If you honestly enjoyed it," Heather looked disgusted as she talked, "then why did you have an exorcism?"

"It was forced on me." Jackie's face darkened. "My parents talked to the local priests, and they tied me to the bed. Did some holy water, prayers, and stuff. I felt him leave the moment they exorcized him out of me. It was like this gaping hole was left in me, and I was normal again. Disgustingly normal." Jackie leaned back roughly in her chair. The two front legs of her seat came off the ground for a moment from the force before clattering back down. "They're the ones making me come here."

"Well, we are glad you're here, Jackie, no matter the reason." Lucy leaned out and touched Jackie's knee lightly for a moment.

The women turned to look at Ruth, "I guess it's my turn." Ruth's hands were balled into fists, grasping the hem of her shirt. "Honestly, I don't really remember much of the possession." She kept her eyes on the floor, "Everything is hazy. It's hard to sleep at night. I have to leave the lights on. I know it sounds stupid, and that light won't keep me safe, but I don't know what to do. Sometimes," Ruth's voice dropped to a whisper, "I feel like I'm being watched, or I have this unnerving feeling that I shouldn't go to the back of my apartment, and that if I do, something horrible will be waiting for me. It only happens when I'm alone." Tears brimmed up in her eyes, "I don't know. Maybe I'm just paranoid now." She wiped away a tear as it started to fall. "I can't talk to my family or friends about it. They wouldn't believe me. I guess I'm just here hoping to not feel alone at the end of the day. I just need someone to believe me and help me through this." Ruth looked at her feet. Her face was hot with embarrassment as another tear escaped across her cheek.

"Then you have come to the right place." Lucy's voice was soft and kind. "When someone goes through intense emotional or physical trauma, like you all have, sometimes they find themselves feeling like it was their fault. Like they are less worthy of companionship and love because of what they have been through. Like they are broken." Lucy looked at each of the members in turn. "This support group will help you find what you have lost in yourselves." Lucy picked up a bag that was by her feet, "Here, I have one for each of you. I would really like you to write down anything that concerns you, or that you remember about the incident. Sometimes it makes it easier to share if you write it down. I know I have trouble finding the right words sometimes when I'm speaking, but for some reason writing flows easier for me." She passed out a composition book to each of the girls. "On the inside of the cover, I taped one of my business cards. You can call me on my cell any time, day or night. I'm here for you if you need anything, ok?" She smiled kindly as she stood up and folded her metal chair. "I think we had a wonderful first meeting today. Will I see you all again on Wednesday? Same time and place?"

The women nodded and folded their chairs, too. They leaned them against the wall where Lucy had placed her own. Ruth gathered her things and started heading towards the door. She felt a little better knowing she wasn't alone in her experiences, but she was mostly just relieved that it was over for today. As she walked out the door, she heard Lucy ask Jackie to stay behind a moment. The only thing that really made Ruth uncomfortable about the meeting now that it was over was Jackie's story.

Ruth drove home in the fading light and climbed the stairs to her apartment. She plopped her purse on the table and laid the notebook down beside it. All of the lights were still on in her place. She was paying almost double the electric bill that she was before the possession, but for her it was a necessary sacrifice. She couldn't stand the thought of walking into a dark room. Ruth walked to her fridge to find something to eat. It was mostly take out boxes of stale Chinese food and half drank soda cans. She pulled out a box of sweet and sour chicken and grabbed a soda from the door of the fridge. Ruth sat down at her kitchen table and flipped open the cover of her notebook.

Lucy's card was taped to the inside cover with her cell number typed in gold lettering. In the center of the card was a fancy design of swirls underlining her name. The bottom of the card had text from a different language that read, "Natas ot gnoleb uoy." Ruth assumed it was something in Latin as she fumbled through her purse for a pen.

She clicked the pen to get it ready to write. "Dear diary." *This is stupid.* Ruth chastised herself as the ink flowed over the paper. She crossed out the words and started again:

"~~Dear diary.~~ I guess let's just get the hard part over with. My name is Ruth Adams, and I was a victim of demonic possession. I don't know why or how, but I do know that it was real. As much as I would like to think that I imagined everything, I didn't. I don't remember much of the actual possession, but I do remember before and after.

Before all of this started, I was fairly happy. Well, maybe not happy, but at least I was content with my life. I first noticed something weird was going on when small items would disappear from where I left them and then reappear in unlikely places. One time, my phone ended up inside the locked trunk of my car. Another time, my sunglasses that I left at work ended up inside of my dresser drawer. It made me feel like I was losing my mind. There was no way I would have put those items there, but at the time, what other explanation could there have been? I seriously thought that I was having psychotic breaks or blackouts. I even contemplated going to a doctor. That's when the scratches started. Long scratches appeared on the insides of my thighs and across my shoulders. It was like my skin was just splitting apart on its own."

Ruth put down the pen. Even just remembering what happened frightened her. Her heart was beating quickly. Her senses were heightened, and the feeling that she was being watched was back. Ruth glanced towards the back bedroom. That's where her instincts told her something bad was waiting. She turned on the T.V. The sound of other human voices helped to alleviate her anxiety. In a way, it tricked her into not feeling so alone. The uncomfortable feeling still nagged at her. Ruth closed her eyes and prayed, "Dear Lord, heavenly father, please watch over me and protect me from evil. Please keep me safe and protect me from any darkness that may try to come near me." Her lips trembled as she whispered the words. A chill ran across her spine. "Grant me strength to overcome evil, and shield me from demons. In your name I pray, amen." The chill dissipated, and the feeling of being watched was gone. Ruth felt a rush of relief. Exhaustion overwhelmed her suddenly. She sat on the edge of the couch and focused on her breathing, trying to get it back to a normal pace. She curled up on the sofa and pulled a thin blanket over herself. Her eyes closed slowly as infomercials played across the television screen.

Ruth stirred awake the next morning. She showered and dressed quickly. She slung her purse over her shoulder and locked the door behind her. The stair well was grey and smelled faintly of Fabuloso and insecticide. Ruth clambered down the stairs until she reached the first floor. She pushed open the door that led to the lobby. White tiles flecked with grey lined the floor. Ruth made her way out of the apartment building towards her car. The city was starting to wake up. Taxis puttered by with visiting business men in the backseats. A woman jogged along the sidewalk, her ponytail swinging behind her. A young man crossed the street with five, small, yappy dogs leading the way on separate leashes. The smell of cigarette smoke and exhaust drifted through the air. Ruth unlocked the door of her car and climbed in. She drove towards the coffee shop she frequented. In her rearview mirror, she saw a black car hanging back. The vehicle stayed back, but it made the same turns she did. Ruth tightened her grip on the steering wheel. She parked near the front of the coffee shop and bolted inside. She watched through the window as the black car drove by slowly. The windows were tinted, so she couldn't see the driver.

"Hey, Ruth!" The girl behind the counter called out, "Want your usual?"

Ruth tucked her hair behind her ear and turned back towards the counter, "Hey, Jules. Yes, please." She smiled halfheartedly and glanced furtively back out the window.

"You doing ok today?" Jules blended some ice cubes into the coffee mixture.

"Yeah, just didn't sleep well."

"Aww, I'm sorry to hear that. Tell you what, why don't you pick out a pastry? On the house." Jules smiled as she mounded whipped cream on top of Ruth's drink.

"Really?" Ruth's face glowed with gratitude at the unexpected gesture of kindness, "Thank you so much. I really appreciate it."

Jules shrugged, "No problem. You're one of my best customers."

Ruth picked out a flaky pastry drizzled with icing and took her to go bag and her drink from Jules. "Have a good day." She lifted her bag as a substitute to waving since her hands were full.

"You, too!" Jules turned to take the next person's order as Ruth headed back to her car.

More cars were starting to edge their way through the city. Ruth pulled out into traffic to make her monotonous morning drive to the office. Traffic trickled past the buildings and sidewalks. Ruth dug her pastry out of the bag she had stashed in the passenger seat. As she took a bite, some icing fell off and landed on her pants. "Crap." Ruth mumbled through a full mouth as she chewed and tried to brush the crumbs off without leaving any residue. Ruth felt her car bump into something. She looked up to see the black car from earlier in front of her. "Oh no." Ruth whispered as she put her car in park and threw on her emergency flashers.

Ruth stepped out of the car, "I'm so sorry, really. I should have watched where I was going."

A middle aged woman climbed out of the car in front of her. She had blonde hair with a scarf tied around her head. She walked to the back of her car where Ruth's bumper was butted up against hers. "I don't think there's any real damage, do you?" She looked up at Ruth.

"No, it...it looks ok." Ruth looked at the woman pleadingly.

"There's no harm done, child, but why don't we exchange numbers and insurance information just in case?" The woman pulled out a small notepad and a pen and looked at Ruth expectantly.

"Ok." Ruth took the pen and paper and scrawled out her number and the name of her insurance company. She passed the notepad back to the woman.

"Wonderful!" She wrote out her own information and tore out a page. She handed the piece of paper to Ruth. The woman grasped one of Ruth's hands in both of her own as Ruth reached out to take the slip of paper. She leaned in and whispered, "You're in danger."

Ruth stared at her for a moment as the woman crawled back into her car and drove away. She looked at the page she held in her hand. There was a number written on it followed by the words, "I'll be in touch." Ruth slid back into the driver's seat, visibly shaken. Why would a stranger tell her that? Was this some kind of sick joke? Ruth started her car and finished her drive to work.

"You're late, Miss Adams." A tall man was leaned against the edge of the receptionist desk. His bald head reflected the fluorescent lights.

"I know. I'm so sorry, Mr. Thompson." Ruth walked around behind the desk and clocked in on her computer. "It won't happen again."

"Could you bring me a print out of my schedule, please?" Mr. Thompson's voice trailed away as he retreated to his office.

"Yes, Sir." Ruth waited for her computer to warm up so she could pull up the list of meetings for today.

The day dragged by. Ruth's thoughts kept running back to the woman from the accident. She was sure it had been the same car that had followed her to the coffee shop. Why would someone want to follow her? What kind of danger was she in? The questions knotted together in the pit of her stomach.

Ruth made her way to the parking lot after work. She was mindful of her surroundings as she drove home. No sign of the black car. She still had a few hours of daylight left as she eased her beat up Toyota into an empty parking spot close to her apartment building. She trudged up the steps and unlocked her apartment. The lights were out.

Ruth scrambled to find the light switch with her fingers. She flicked the switch and the light came on. Her heart pounded as she eased into the room. Darkness bled from the back of the apartment. Everything looked untouched except for the lights. Ruth went around to the kitchen, bathroom, and living room flipping on all of the light switches. The ominous feeling was being exuded from the back room again. Ruth backed into the lighted area of the living room. Terror coursed through her. She flipped on the T.V. to distract herself. *It's ok.* Ruth tried to calm herself down. *You're ok. Just breathe.* Her heart was still racing, but her breathing was more even now. She walked over to the kitchen table and picked up the pen again.

"After the scratches started forming on my body, I realized that what was happening was like something out of a horror movie. I called a psychic from the want ads to come over, but she wouldn't even come in the apartment. Her face turned pale when I opened the door, and she fled. I didn't want to call my friends or family. They don't believe in spirits. Honestly, at first I thought it was just a ghost. I had done some research online, and poltergeists seemed to be the top result for what I was experiencing.

I booked a hotel room, hoping that it was just attached to something in the apartment, but that didn't help. I woke up in the middle of the night with blood soaking into the sheets and the mattress of the bed. I could feel it sticking to my thighs and my calves. I tried to scream, but it was like all of the air was being driven into my body. I think that's when it really took hold of me.

I don't remember much after that, just flashes of places. I saw my work. I saw my apartment. I saw the outside of the local hospital. Mostly I just remember the smell of rotten eggs when I would come to my senses momentarily. The smell mixed with the intense heat of its presence in a cloud of stifling despair. I couldn't make sense of time or even really the glimpses of things that I saw. It felt like I was drowning constantly in a sea of darkness.

Later, I found out it was the psychic that had told the priests where I lived. She was reason they came to check on me, and honestly, she may be the only reason I'm even still alive at this point."

Ruth put down the pen. The hairs on her arms were standing on end. It felt as though cold fingers had just trailed along the back of her neck. Ruth shivered as goosebumps spread along her body. She shuffled to the fridge and pulled out a bottle of vodka. *Just something to calm my nerves.* Ruth let the chilled liquid burn her throat as she took a swig. The glass bottle clinked against her teeth as she tilted it back down. The alcohol left a trail of fire down her esophagus and into her stomach.

She curled up on the couch as a car dealership commercial flashed its latest deals across the T.V. Ruth tucked her knees closer to her chest and pulled the wrinkled blanket around her. She closed her eyes as the vodka worked its way into her system. Her empty stomach sped up her body's absorption. Her arms and legs started to feel lighter as she drifted off into an intoxicated sleep.

Her dreams were plagued with the screams of babies and figures that darted through the shadows. Ruth could feel fingers entangled in her long hair. Strands of her hair tugged against her scalp. She could feel them rip away from her head. She tried to disentangle herself from where her hair was caught, but the fingers jolted closed and yanked her backwards. The skin on her heels grated against gravel. She struggled to find footing, but the force dragging her was too strong. Suddenly, the ground dropped from beneath her. Ruth plummeted in the darkness; her hair fluttered around her face. Her stomach did flips as she fought to catch her breath.

Ruth's eyes opened as she woke up. She looked around herself. She was on the floor. Her blanket was tangled around her ankles. Her hair was matted with sweat. Early morning television flashed by cheerily in the grey light that seeped through the curtains. She breathed a sigh of relief as she picked herself up off the dusty floor. Cleaning had been put on the back burner lately. She pulled herself to her feet and walked to the shower.

Steam filled the air around her as lavender soap bubbles swirled down the drain. The water helped. It felt clean and safe as she detangled her hair. A clump came out between her fingers. Ruth pulled her hand away, starring at the strands that clung to her palm. She wadded up the ball of hair and stashed it behind the shampoo bottle. Ruth turned off the water and dried herself off. There weren't any visible bald patches. She kneaded her scalp with her finger tips. It was tender to the touch. She got dressed quickly and shoved the notebook in her purse.

Work was monotonous. Clients and schedules and cancelations. The day dragged on until it was finally time to leave the office. Ruth caught herself absentmindedly massaging her scalp throughout the day. It was still sore. She climbed in her car and turned the key. The next meeting would be starting soon. Ruth drove to the orphanage and made her way inside.

Her footsteps echoed down the deserted hall. Ruth opened the door to the room where they met last time. Only Lucy and Jackie were there. The other girls hadn't show up yet. The chairs were already set up. Ruth took the same seat she had last time and placed her purse in her lap. She still wasn't entirely comfortable, especially with Jackie around.

"How are you doing, Ruth?" Lucy looked at her tenderly.

"I had a rough night sleep." Ruth rubbed her scalp.

Lucy clicked her tongue, "Nightmares?"

"Yeah." Ruth looked her a little suspiciously.

"It's normal to experience nightmares when you go through a trauma." A small smile played across her lips, "It's typically just your subconscious trying to make sense of everything that happened to you."

The door opened, and Brandy and Heather walked in. Heather looked over her shoulder, "Did you guys see the blonde in the scarf when you came in?"

"What blonde?" Lucy's voice was a little harsher than she intended.

"Some lady outside." Brandy jerked her thumb towards the front of the building.

"How old did she look?" Ruth was staring at Brandy.

Brandy paused for a moment, "Probably mid to late forties."

"You should all be very careful." Lucy's eyes darted to each of them and her brow furrowed with worry. "We aren't really in the best part of town, and you never know what kind of people are lurking about. You should be especially careful since you are all still very vulnerable."

"What do you mean? Why vulnerable?" Brandy was fiddling nervously with her bracelets.

Lucy looked to Heather who took a deep breath. Heather touched the tiny cross that dangled around her neck, "Your soul is just like any other part of your body. When it gets banged around, it needs time to heal. During an exorcism, the demon who is inhabiting the possessed person clings onto the soul. The priest has to basically rip the demon off of the soul. That—combined with the stress of being inhabited initially—leaves it weak and, well," Heather turned towards Lucy, "vulnerable."

"Exactly." Lucy nodded.

"My dad has actually had multiple patients that have been repossessed after he has performed exorcisms on them. A lot of times they think that he just didn't really get the demon out, but he says it's more like there is a mark on the soul. There's a darkness that draws the evil back to them." Heather sat down softly in her chair.

"So we basically have targets on backs." Brandy scrunched her hair between her fingers as she let out a frustrated sigh and dropped into the empty chair beside Heather.

"On your souls, but yes." Lucy looked at them gravely, "Just please be very careful. Especially if you have all seen this woman lurking about." Her face looked grim and frightened as she looked towards the door, "You never know who might be working against you." Lucy shook her head as if to clear away unwanted thoughts, "Why don't we get back on track?" Her normal smile replaced the tight-lipped frown. "Everyone take your seats. Who would like to share first today?"

"I'll go." It was the first time Jackie had spoken since the meeting began. "I wanted to apologize for the other day. I've been doing a lot of soul searching the past few days, and I think maybe I was just interested in being special. It didn't matter where that came from, as long as I had it." Jackie looked at the floor in embarrassment. "I just wanted to feel like I was a part of something bigger than myself, and having the demon inside me gave me the power to overcome the other things in my life. My home life isn't great. My older brother died when I was thirteen. He was always the golden boy...the one that did everything perfectly." Jackie shuffled her shoes against the floor, "After he died, nothing I could do was good enough. I was living the shadow of a dead person. Everything I did was measured up to his perfect standards. So," Jackie chipped away at her black nail polish, "I decided that if I was never going to be as good as he was, then I was going to be as bad as they played me out to be. I really got into Ouija boards when I was about fourteen. I prayed to Satan every night. I even tried to contact my demonic guardian a few times. It's kind of like a guardian angel, but for the other team." She looked up at the group, "Part of me didn't really believe in it if I'm being honest, but another part always hoped."

"You're a part of this now." Lucy smiled at Jackie warmly, "And we only want you to be you. As cliché as that sounds." She laughed, and it was like tiny bells tinkling. Ruth still felt a little uneasy about Jackie. It seemed like too much of a turnaround for just two days.

"Are we seriously just going to sit here and talk about our feelings instead of doing something?" Brandy ran her fingers through her hair.

"My dad sent me a care package from the Philippines." Heather sat up straighter.

"Good for you, princess." Brandy's agitation bubbled up as she threw a look at Heather.

Heather glared at her, "What I mean is, he's been doing exorcisms over there." She turned back to the rest of the group, "The package had a St. Benedict Crucifix in it and a few bottles of holy water. It also had some Sina Ginger Candy, but I don't think that will help us right now." Heather touched the cross at her throat again as she thought about her dad, "He knows I'm still struggling, and a care package is really the only way he can help me while he's gone."

"That's great." Lucy looked at Heather sympathetically. "Is it in your car?"

"No." Heather shook her head. "It's back at my house."

"Ok, well, why don't you go get it and meet us back here? I think that might make us all feel a little better." Lucy nodded as she spoke.

"Wait!" Ruth called out as Heather began to gather her things. "I don't think you should go alone. It's not safe out there."

"I agree." Lucy's face contorted in concern. "Jackie? Would you go with Heather?"

"Of course." Jackie agreed instantly.

"Oh, no, really," Heather stammered, "I'll be ok."

"Please?" Jackie reached out and touched Heather's arm, "Please, just give me a chance."

Heather paused, looking into Jackie's pleading eyes. She breathed out and nodded her head, "Okay."

Ruth watched as the two of them left the room. She still didn't trust Jackie. Doubt bubbled up in her stomach. "What do we do now?" Ruth's voice came out in a whisper.

"Well," Lucy scooted her chair closer into the circle. The legs scraped along the floor with a drawn-out squeak. "We can still talk."

"I'm gonna go take a piss." Brandy placed her hands on her knees and pushed off.

Lucy waited for the door to click shut behind her as Brandy went to find a bathroom, hopefully one with working plumbing. "It's sad. Some people only want to believe in a higher power when things are looking up." She turned back to Ruth. Her blonde hair framed her face. "Do you want to talk about your nightmares?"

"Not really." Ruth looked at the floor.

"You don't want to know what happened to the babies?"

Ruth's eyes shot up, "What?" Her breath caught in her throat.

"Oh, you know." Lucy stood up and walked behind her chair. She let her fingers trail along the back of it. Her manner was almost seductive. "The ones whose screams you hear at night." Ruth's fingers trembled as Lucy laughed. "Think back to those small little bundles of joy you took so easily from the hospital. Do you remember the way their soft flesh felt against your fingertips? The way their heads needed support?" Lucy mimed holding a baby. "The littlest one grabbed your pinkie. Do you remember his tiny hand? His pink smell?"

Ruth was shaking, "Who are you?"

"No, no, no, let's not rush our time." Lucy clicked her tongue like the ticking of a clock. "I want you to close your eyes and remember."

"I don't—"

"Uh, uh, uh," Lucy wagged her finger, "Eyes closed."

Ruth unwillingly closed her eyes, "I don't remember anything from when—"

"Let me set the scene." Lucy walked soundlessly behind Ruth and crouched so that she could whisper in her ear. "It was a clear night. There was a cool breeze. You were standing on top of a bridge. You could smell the water. The little brats were nestled in the back seat. Then, ever so carefully, you picked them up, one by one, and tossed them over the edge." Lucy's voice escalated in terrifying joy.

"No." A tear slid down Ruth's cheek. Distorted images ran across her eyelids: headlights, a baby blanket, rippling water. "It wasn't me!" Ruth's eyes flared open. "It was whatever was inside of me." Rage and self-hatred flooded through her.

"Ha!" Lucy laughed, "You're too pretty for such copouts. No, it was you. We just helped you do what you always wanted to do." Lucy looked slyly at Ruth, "You were my inspiration for choosing this place, you know. The place that turned you down when you wanted to adopt." Lucy savored every word.

"I *never* wanted to hurt children." Ruth's fingernails dug into her palms.

"No, but you were jealous." Lucy licked her lips, "All those fertility treatments, the sperm donors, because no one could stand your paranoia long enough to get you pregnant the old fashioned way. You're a burden, but you already knew that. That's why you didn't call your family when things started getting really hairy." Lucy pouted, "And even with all the medical marvels they have, you were still barren. Your womb as empty of life as your life was empty of meaning." She spun on her heel with a flourish, "Quite poetic, really. Maybe the universe just knew you would make a terrible mother, and judging by what you did on the top of that bridge, the universe was right."

"Stop it!" Ruth was rocking back and forth as the tears fell freely. She raised her hands to cover her ears, but Lucy only talked louder.

"And you decided that if you couldn't have a baby, then no one would." She punctuated the last four words by shifting her hips from side to side.

"No." Ruth whispered between her sobs. The door shook as if someone was trying to get in.

"Go Away!" Lucy screeched, spinning to face the doorway. Her shoulders hunched up like an animal. She turned back to Ruth, "You are the weakest one. You know that right?" She crossed her arms and leaned down condescendingly. "Look at you. You're pathetic. Crying like a—whoops, I almost said 'baby.'" Lucy cackled.

"If I'm so pathetic," Ruth looked up through tear-matted lashes, "then why even bother?"

"Why, because, darling. You may be pathetic, but you're mine." Lucy ran her finger down Ruth's hair. Ruth pulled away from her.

The door burst open. Lucy growled as she flung her wrist toward the entrance. An empty chair flew towards the door and slammed into Brandy's chest, knocking the wind out of her. Heather stepped over Brandy's limp body followed by the woman in the scarf. Heather had a crucifix in her hand. The woman was evoking angels and praying vehemently. She carried a large, black gun.

"What?" Lucy laughed mockingly, "You think I'm afraid of a gun? I was forged in hellfire, molded with sulfur, and sculpted by time." Her voice deepened as she spoke. The bell-like quality was gone.

The woman kept praying. She aimed the weapon at Lucy. A stream of water surged forth as Lucy's new baritone voice laughed, shaking the window panes with its vibrations. The laughter was cut short as the water hit her face and sizzled against her skin. She squealed in pain and turned away. Ruth could see blisters bubbling to the surface of her cheek and across her left eye.

"Holy water." Heather brandished her crucifix higher. The two women continued approaching steadily.

A growl erupted from Lucy's throat as she twitched her wrist again. Another chair flew from the circle and collided with the scarfed woman's head. A loud smack echoed as she slumped to the floor. Lucy jerked her head to the side. Her neck cracked into a strange angle as she turned her attention to Heather. A toothy grin split across her face.

"Lucifer! In the name of the Father, I expel you! In the name of the Son, I expel you!" Lucy lunged at Heather's throat with her teeth, "In the name of the Holy Spirit, I expel you!" Heather screamed the words with conviction as Lucy's teeth scraped against her skin.

Lucy's body convulsed on the ground. White spit bubbles foamed at the corners of her mouth, and her eyes rolled back into her head. The blisters on her face were swollen with liquid, almost to the point of bursting. Lucy's arms thrashed against the floor. Her head jerked back in one last contraction before a slow exhale wheezed out of her lips. The body went limp.

Ruth walked over to the body slowly, "Is it over?"

"Yes." Heather placed her fingers on Lucy's neck. "No pulse." She looked up at Ruth.

The woman wearing the scarf stirred and sucked air through her teeth. She winced as she sat up and touched her head. Her fingers came away bloody. "She's been dead for a while." The woman stood up and walked over to the girls. "When Satan takes over a body, it's different than when a lesser demon inhabits someone." She wobbled as she tried to maintain her balance. Heather grabbed her elbow to help support her. "Satan takes up more room and burns hotter. The host's soul can't last very long under those conditions."

"Who are you?" Ruth was still trembling as she looked at the woman.

"Well," The woman reached up and straightened her scarf, "I used to be called Sister Mary Eucharist. Now though, I just go by Angela."

"She used to be a nun." Heather helped Angela to one of the chairs that hadn't been flung around the room and then went to check on Brandy. She talked over her shoulder as she helped Brandy sit up. "She saved me when I got outside with Jackie."

"Where is Jackie?" Ruth looked through the doorway trying to catch a glimpse of her.

"Knocked out on the sidewalk." Angela pulled off her scarf and used it to dab at the blood coming from her head. "She had already been repossessed."

"I think it happened when Lucy asked her to stay late at the last meeting." Heather held up her index finger, and Brandy was following it back and forth with her eyes. "She certainly seemed up for another possession last time." Heather shook her head.

"She'll be ok, but I don't think her body can take another possession." Angela pulled her scarf away and looked at the blood. Her cut was starting to clot. "She's battered, but I don't think that will stop her from opening herself up to evil again." She shook her head.

"Did you know about all this when I hit your car?" Ruth's breath was coming quicker. She was on the verge of a panic attack. Her eyes darted back and forth.

"One of the gifts of the Holy Spirit is discernment." Angela looked at Ruth intently, "And you, child, have such a darkness hanging over you." She tilted her head. I knew something was after you, but I didn't know it was this serious. I followed you. I saw the other girls with the same darkness hovering above them. When I saw the dark haired girl walking out with this one," she gestured to Heather, I took my chance. The demon in her told us about Lucifer's great plan. Demons like to brag, one of their downfalls."

"Do you always carry an exorcism kit with you?" Ruth looked at the water gun leaking on the floor.

Angela smiled, "Honey, when you've seen all the stuff that I've seen, you stay prepared."

Brandy groaned, and Heather helped her up. Ruth lowered her voice, "Do they lie?"

"The demons?" Angela brushed her hair away from her face. "They don't have to lie. They can see into the darkest parts of your soul. That's their way in. The truth is far uglier and more terrifying than any lie could ever be."

Tears streamed down Ruth's face. The images of the babies were seared into her mind now. Vomit seared her throat as she retched on the floor.

Angela stood up and walked over to Ruth. She rubbed her back as Ruth spit up more stomach acid. "Honey, whatever it is you did, God can forgive you if you ask him." Ruth shook her head no and dug her fingernails into her thighs. "Yes, yes, he can." Angela nodded. "Demonic possession brings out the worst in people. You did not have complete control of yourself. Listen to me, they can take even the tiniest seed of evil in your heart and grow it into a terrible force of nature." She stroked Ruth's hair. "What is important now is that you ask forgiveness and live in the light. Just make the most of what time you have left here." Ruth turned and rested her forehead on Angela's shoulder. "Would you like me to pray for you?" Angela's voice was soft and comforting as Ruth nodded. "Our Father, who art in heaven, hallowed be thy name. We humbly come before you to thank you for this victory today and ask for your help once again." Ruth felt Heather place her hand on her shoulder as Angela prayed. "Please bless this broken child and help mend the wounds, both spiritual and physical that have been left behind by this attack. Surround her with your love and grace, and give her the strength to make it through this trial in her life. Lord, we know you only give us what we can handle, and judging by the amount of tribulation you have placed on this girl, you must think she is so strong." Ruth felt Brandy's hand rest on her other shoulder. "Help us to stay on your path, and may your will be done on Earth as it is in heaven." Brandy and Heather joined Angela in unison, "Amen."

"Amen." Ruth whispered. Some of the weight lifted off of her chest as she pulled away and looked at the three of them. "Thank you."

The days to come were marked by depression for Ruth. She struggled with the torment of what she had done. The nightmares persisted. She, Brandy, and Heather attended survivor meetings led by Angela every Saturday. Brandy eventually got a job as a photographer. She found that spending her life behind the camera gave her more joy than her time in front of it. Some of her clients recognized her from her porn career, but mostly that just helped to put them more at ease with her. The old adage of 'imagine your audience naked' was just a little easier for them. Heather's father came back from the Philippines, and she joined him in performing exorcisms. She often joked that after exorcising Satan, lesser demons were a piece of cake. She helped to calm the patients, but in the meetings she confessed she was still terrified during every session. Angela mentored the girls and did her best to help them with their own struggles. Jackie died a few weeks after they performed her second exorcism. They found a business card beside her body with the text 'Natas ot gnoleb uoy' typed in gold. Under the text, Jackie had sloppily scribbled the words backwards and in reverse order: you belong to Satan. Her eyes could not be closed, and her cracked lips were peeled back in a toothy grin. Her family chose not to have an open casket.

THE SCARRED

TINA FORTH

She wasn't always called Narla. In her past, she was known by another name and lived in a forest made of stone on an island off the coast of a vast land. Narla couldn't remember much about those days. They seemed hazy in her mind, because many winters had passed by her since she lived in the stone city. She thought of herself as Narla and it was all that mattered.

Narla liked to sit in her favorite tree in the forest and watch the vultures soar high in the sky. Those beautiful birds spent the entire afternoon in the up there and barely flapped a wing. She remembered the time one of them tried to land on a cliff and missed it four times. Each time the magnificent bird would return for another pass until it finally found a place to land. The vultures were her friends. She knew they watched out for her and let her know when there was danger in the forest. If she followed them, they would show her things to eat.

She'd lived in the forest ever since the night she was taken to it by the tribe. The tribe consisted of very bad people who did horrible things to women. Narla remembered when she lived in the stone city and knew people like her. Those days were long gone, but she was happy. So long as she could find food and a safe place to sleep, she was very happy. There were bears and wolves in the forest, but she'd learned to avoid them. Bears could be sent running if you hit them in the nose with a stone.

That day, Narla sat on the branch of her favorite tree and watched the birds on the end of her limb. She was hungry and the birds had a nest of eggs. Those eggs would keep her fed for another day. Narla didn't mind if she spent the entire morning near the nest. All she needed to do was sit in place and the birds would forget she was there. The birds might smell her, but Narla took care to roll in some pinesap before she climbed the trees that day. The forest was mostly pine in this part and the birds wouldn't notice her smell. She sat there on the branch and held a place with her feet. Her hands grabbed the branch on which she perched. Every hour she advanced another foot toward the nest. The birds didn't notice even when the branch slipped down each time she moved toward them.

Sometimes Narla would remember the tribe and what they did to her. How she was grabbed from the stone city and taken to the forest. So much was blank in her mind. All she needed to know, she remembered. But every so often, she would remember the tribe and what it had done to her. How each of them did horrible things and dumped her in the forest. The worst was when the man hit her in the head with a rock. Narla almost died the first week as she wondered around senseless. Then she found some wild onions and they tasted good.

"I swear to God," Robert said to Bo as they walked down the trail, "that crazy lady is somewhere out here. I know because I've seen her in the past." He turned and peered at a shadow in the tree line, but it was just a limb.

"That's what you said about the ghost of Matilda Gray," Bo snapped back at him. "Didn't you say she came one night and threatened to kill you? Didn't you tell us this is why you married her daughter?"

"Different situation," Robert replied. "It was the only way her daughter would ever consent to marry me. So I played on her superstitions." Every man in the hunting party had a laugh.

There were five of them in Northwestern Pennsylvania that afternoon. Hunting season had begun and they could take time off from their work to look for deer. All of them carried shotguns, although Howard brought along a rifle from the European War. They'd been up late that night distilling off the last of the hooch for the buyer who was supposed to pick it up from them in a week for his speakeasy. Business was good and there were plenty of people who wanted it, even if congress had banned the sale of alcoholic beverages in the United States. So long as Wall Street made everyone rich, there was no reason to keep out of the party.

Bo was out in the front. At twenty-eight, he was the leader of the band and knew how to make the hooch. Buck was his brother and two years younger. Robert knew about the process of fermenting a batch of corn and found them a campsite in the woods to use. David was a cousin who was twenty and wanted in on the operation. The last member of their party was Howard, who was from another branch of the family in Maine. They had a nice little operation hidden away in the woods on the other side of the mountain and didn't worry about anyone interfering with it.

They didn't know that Howard was with the federal government.

The revenue men had tracked the illegal booze operation, which supplied so much jackleg whiskey to Pittsburgh months ago. It was a serious matter to have one of their people on the inside. This was not easy to do since most of these local families went back generations and didn't talk much to outsiders. Howard was one of Mr. Hoover's new men who rose up through the ranks and had a spotless record. When the chance came to infiltrate a bootlegging operation in Pennsylvania, he jumped at the opportunity.

"So how do you know so much about this crazy lady?" Howard asked Robert. "It sounds like you're some kind of expert." He played the role of an out-of-state relative who needed work and wasn't too bright.

"Because I was one of the men Sheriff Sanders deputized to find her," he told his friends. "Back when that lady from the city disappeared around here. You know, the lady whose purse they found near the reservoir."

Howard nodded as if he knew a little bit, but not much. In fact, Howard the government agent worked on that case. The local county contacted Washington for help as she was from a family of quality and it made them all look bad at the courthouse. Poor little rich girl goes missing from the streets of Pittsburgh. Her car is found in a forest near the North West Pennsylvania federal land (another reason to call Washington). Government men swoop all over the woods, but they don't find a thing. Another mysterious disappearance for the history books.

Howard knew more about the case than he wanted to admit. It broke his heart when he found out what happened and who did it. He didn't like to think much about it. Many years had gone by since it happened.

Narla was about to move forward on her branch when she saw the tribe move below her. What was this? The tribe never ventured into her forest, they knew what would happen. This was her land and she protected everything in it. She stood still and became a part of the tree as the tribesmen moved under her on the old trail. There were only a few of them. It caused her to remember the night she was taken to the forest. It was men like the ones below Narla who did those things to her.

She stopped her observation of them and tried to remember what happened. Something about trusting them and why she'd let them take her to this place. She felt funny in the head and crept back to the tree. The birds noticed her, but she wasn't very hungry all of the sudden. Narla held onto the tree trunk and became part of it as she watched the tribe slide past her position and vanish into the forest.

This was her forest and she would defend it. The naked young woman slipped down from the tree and hid behind a bush. She didn't resemble anything civilized, with her long tattered hair and mud-covered skin. Narla didn't appear to be anything human. She dropped to the ground, whistling like a bird just in case anyone looked in her direction, and began to circle around the tribesmen. She could follow them until the time was right to act.

The sharp knife was still under the rock where she left it. Narla found it last year foraging through the old cabin. It held a good edge and she used it as a tool. Lashed to a stick, it was excellent for catching fish. She took it out of its hiding place and moved back to where she saw the tribe on the move. Soon they would leave unless they planned to stay here. She still hadn't decided what to do about them.

Then Narla saw the man with the stick in the back of the column. She remembered that stick. Narla recalled a man who held it to her head while the others did things to her. Her thoughts were garbled and she couldn't remember much about what happened afterward, but the stick she did remember. It made loud sounds and she was scarred of it.

If he held the stick, it must be the same man who caused her so much pain. Then she noticed all the tribesmen carried sticks. These had to be the same men who dumped her in these woods years ago. Narla ran her finger along the sharp blade of her knife. There was a sickness in the forest and she needed to cut it out.

"Is this the place you talked about?" Bo said to Robert. "The way you talked, I thought it was some kind of palace.

"Just an old cabin," Robert replied. He was the biggest man out of the party but didn't eat all that much.

David propped his shotgun against the tree outside and looked at the old cabin. It still had a roof, but the entrance didn't have a door on it. There was a small porch, but he did trust the eaves over it. Howard, his rifle cradled under his arm, walked into the cabin and looked around. Not much left, hard to say who built it or why.

Howard tried to look his most innocent. They'd accepted him as one of the family all week and he'd done his best to earn their trust as he helped them distill the hooch. Several barrels were already in the back of the truck at the other camp. No one would bother it while they were out here. No one was supposed to know about the other camp. All he needed to do was contact someone in Washington when they left the camp and it would be cleaned-up. He didn't like betraying these men, but there were laws. Plus, he wanted that promotion.

They decided to make camp in front of the cabin as no one wanted to sleep inside it. The men unpacked their bedrolls and put up some canvas overhead just in case it rained. It was going to be a good weekend of hunting before they had to get back to the stock. Howard joined them around the fire and made up a few tales of fishing in Maine to keep them interested. However, for the most part, he allowed them to talk while he remained silent. They gave him useful evidence he could use later.

They found David's body in the morning. Bo got up first that morning to get the fire started and went out to take a piss after it was going. He'd dropped his pants when he noticed a boot that stuck out from behind a tree. After he buttoned his pants, Bo crunched through the old undergrowth to see who it was. They'd all had a bit too much of the stock last night and assumed it was one of the crew.

"So which one of you...." he started to say before he looked down and saw David slumped up against the tree with his throat cut out. His blood was dry, as it had drained hours ago.

The best they could figure was that it happened sometime in the night. Howard didn't want to give his cover away, but he could tell it was done with a knife. A big one, given the slash marks. It was quick and David never had the chance to scream.

"The crazy lady," Bo said as they stared down at the body.

It didn't take Narla long to take care of the first member of the tribe. He was foolish. All she needed to do was sit and wait for someone to venture outside of their camp that night. She stood perfectly still all evening in her most stone pose. Narla perfected the pose the first year she lived in the forest. For a week after she came to the forest, Narla sat in one spot and did not move. She drank the water from the rain and managed to chew on some food she had with her. Her weight dropped quickly, but she didn't care. Inside her mind, she was dead and waited to fade into nothingness. Eventually, she did become nothing. After the week of sitting in the same place, she began to move. Just a little bit. Then she moved enough to crawl across the ground and find something to eat. It wasn't hard; she seemed to know what plants were good for her and which ones would bring instant death.

Narla became something between animal and human that crept on the ground to survive and hid in the dark. She located a cave to stay inside when the weather was bad and soon taught her how to crawl up a tree when a bear threatened her. She had no sense of who she was or what she'd been. All such information was gone, stolen from her when the men took her into the woods. The rock to the head was the final thing that caused her to lose her sense of self. They'd left her for dead, but she became something else. None of the men thought she was still alive or they'd have taken care of her earlier.

As she grew stronger, Narla learned to steal food and clothes from the farms near the forest. Stories spread of a wild woman who lived in the forest and hunters were told to watch out for her. Other people confused her with a woman who lost her mind and ran off into the forest, never to be seen again. Narla had a keen sense of danger by now and would vanish up a tree or into a grove if she heard anything, which suggested the tribe to her. Other people were always the tribe to her, as she had no other concept of them.

But this group was different. There was something about them that brought back the memories of what sent her to the forest. She knew they would contaminate the forest and kill the only place she knew as home. Narla wasn't about to allow that to happen. As she watched, the others gather around the dead body on the ground, she ran her thumb along the knife blade again and waited. They might try to leave, but they still had her to consider.

"His throat cut ear-to-ear," Bo said the rest of the group. "Who would do this? Your crazy lady wouldn't know how. This has to be the work of those boys from Slippery Rock."

There was another gang of bootleggers from Slippery Rock who wanted to muscle in on their hooch operation. Howard knew about them from his office in New York City. Many of these small-timer operations were consolidating in the wake of increased pressure from the federals. It made sense as a way to save and hide materials when the government constantly tried to locate them. Howard adjusted his jacket and scanned the area with concentration. Somehow, he didn't think it was the rival gang, but he couldn't let them know his reasons.

"I don't think it's the Slippery Rock gang," Robert said as he looked at the body. "They wouldn't have used a knife. That bunch would have taken us all out at once. They brought back those Thompsons from the war and like to use them."

"We need to get out of here," Buck said to the rest of the band. "There could be more of them in the woods just waiting to kill us all. And what about the stock we left at our camp? If these are the Slippery Rock Boys, they'll go right for it. We'd be left with our pants down and nothing to deliver to the buyers." He picked up his shotgun and loaded two shells into it.

"Yeah," Bo agreed. "We need to get moving." He gave orders, just like in the war, to the other men to break camp and head back to the base.

"No reason to stay here another night," he told them. "And keep a watch for any strange movement out there. Some of these old boys know the woods just as good as we do."

Howard kept his eyes on the terrain at all times while he rolled up his blanket. He didn't think it was the rival gang. Just not their style. Someone wanted to send them a message. Perhaps it was the crazy lady they talked about, but crazy people seldom had the mental reasoning to carry out a murder such as this. It appeared to be the style of someone who wanted to see them all gone or dead. Howard worried the second option was what they had in mind.

"Has anyone seen Buck?" Bo asked them, as they made ready to leave. The group packed everything quick and was ready to go in an hour. Buck wanted to take the body with them, but Bo overruled him and said it was a matter for the sheriff, who was in their pocket. He'd let the sheriff know where the body could be found after they delivered the hooch. They would give David's share to his family. Let the law deal with whoever killed him. They would have to move their operations and the law could make things bad for Slippery Rock. Besides, everyone just wanted to get out of there.

Narla watched them break camp and prepare to leave. The memories of what happened to her continued to flood her mind and she had a hard time to remain still on the tree branch where she watched them.

Yesterday's kill was easy. He didn't even see her until she came up behind him and touched his shoulder. It was so much easier than a deer or bear as the tribesman didn't even have fur over most of his body. One slash and he went down. She was careful to aim her cut right below his face to do the most damage.

When he went down, Narla wondered what to do about him. The body wasn't of much use to her and she didn't want to cause the others to scatter until the sun came up. She finally decided the man was best displayed in a way that would scare the others away from the forest. Narla spent an hour or so arranging the body in the best way possible. She even placed flowers all over him to let the others know it wasn't a bear. Bears didn't hurt people too often, but they had no way to know it.

From her spot on the limb, she waited until one of the tribesmen would move in her range. She watched one of them argue with a man who appeared to be in charge. The rest packed and wanted to leave in a hurry. This wasn't what Narla wanted. She wanted them to be scared and terrified of her. She wanted these men to know who was responsible and let the others know it would happen to them if they ever moved into the forest where she lived. She only needed one of them to survive and tell the others.

Narla hopped down the tree limbs. She noticed one man had left the larger party and went back the body for some reason. He seemed to be angry. She didn't want two of them in the same place and it would be hard to carry off any one of them. It was better the bodies be spaced out for maximum effect. This wasn't too much of a problem since they were all ready to move and this would make it easy for her.

Buck was headed back to the location of David's body when he heard something hit the dirt behind him. He spun around with the shotgun, terrified it was one of the gang come back to finish the rest of them off. He didn't see a thing behind him. Dammit, what kind of family would they be to leave David's body back there to be chewed up by the animals?

One of his uncles died in the woods years ago and they still talked about how disgusting he looked when he was found.

Relieved there was nothing behind him, Buck adjusted his wool cap and turned back to the trail. He planned to haul David's body back himself and tell the sheriff it was an accident. They could take care of the matter in the family and not have to involve outsiders. What kind of family was it where you had to bring in the law for what they needed to handle on your own? The law would make things worse for them. He began to hum and continued to the tree where David's body was left.

Buck stopped. There was a pile of leaves in front of him. It blocked the trail. This wasn't right; there had been anything in the middle of the trail when they went to examine David's body the first time. He stopped and looked at the pile. It wasn't very big and hugged the ground. Could some animal have swept it out here? Was it the wind? He went over and gave the pile a gentle kick, expecting it to move off the trail.

The pile of leaves grabbed his ankle and pulled him to the ground.

Out of the leaf pile, a figure emerged with mud for a body and matted hair for a head. Buck was terrified by the vision in front of him and froze. When it moved in his direction, he tried to find his shotgun, but it was too late. Narla was on top of him in seconds.

Buck tried to push the demon off him, but she held onto his arm and had the advantage of surprise. Narla brought her knife down in an arch and stabbed Buck through the eye and into his brain. The last thing she saw was a tiny woman coated with dirt who plunged a knife into him. Buck gagged and was silent.

Narla looked down at him as she wiped off her blade on his shirt. Next, she looked up and wondered how long it would take his friends to notice he was gone. Probably not, long. This would be the first place they'd look once someone noticed he wasn't with the rest of the group.

She wanted to prepare him as she'd don't the other, but the flowers were out of the question. Narla drug him across the trail and positioned him on one of the many trees. She took out her knife and carved a pretty shape several times over him. This would let the rest of them know who did it. Hadn't they told her how much she was loved when they got her into the car? She placed one hand on her head and tried to remember some more thoughts, but they were all so hard to recall.

Robert was the one who took off first to find Buck. Bo watched him leave and then decided they all should accompany him. It was obvious Buck went back to get David's body since he was no fan of leaving him.

"I need to explain a few things to him," he grumbled with the others who trailed behind. "I'm in charge here and he is going to do as I...."

And then they found the body of Buck.

"A knife again," Bo, said to the rest of the men as they glanced nervously at the trees. "Maybe you all will listen to me in the future. We have to get out of here now and don't ask me about what to do with this body." The men began to back out of the trail and headed in the direction of the broken campsite.

Howard looked the body over carefully before he left. Who would care Valentine's hearts into the body of a victim?

Narla was very still again as the tribesmen came upon the body of the man she'd killed. She didn't know if the leaf pile trick would work with him. It had with the bears and rabbits, but she didn't know how much the tribesmen used smell to track their pray. She'd seen them move around in the past and didn't understand how they found game. She used her eyes and sense of observation. The larger animals relied on smell a lot, but she could always out think them if she had to do it.

Narla watched them move away quicker this time. It didn't surprise her; they wanted to get away from her, even if they didn't know where she was at the time. The only thing Narla had going for her was her stealth. She was half the size of most of those men and couldn't engage them in a direct fight. However, like with the bears, she didn't have to fight them if she wanted to kill one.

She let them get far enough down the trail before she left her perch on the tree limb. Narla could smell the fear from them, which was good for her. She decided to wait before she struck again. It would take them a few hours to get out of her forest. In a few hours, they would become complacent again and she could strike once more. She had to be careful of those sticks they carried that made such a loud noise. She's seen what they could do in the past and didn't want to be on the receiving end of it.

This time she followed them on the ground. The forest was quiet, but there were always plenty of animals in the background. She watched them use their sticks at a fox, but it was too fast for them. One of the tribesmen grabbed a man who'd used his stick too quick and an argument ensued.

Hours later, one of the tribesmen fell back. He was a little bit tired and couldn't keep up with the rest. Narla crept closer and closer each time, careful to avoid the sticks on the ground that might snap. All the years she'd lived in the forest taught her to watch out for anything that could make any noise. Several times, she nearly starved after losing a rabbit when it heard her in the background. She crawled after the tribe on the ground and smelled the rich sent of soil as she went along. It was an odor that always managed to comfort her.

Howard was scared.

In all the years he'd worked as a government agent he'd never felt such terror. He was ready to tell the others who he really was, but they would kill him on the spot. Even if he took them out first, he'd still have to contend with whoever had killed the two men. Someone or something wanted them all dead. This couldn't be the work of a rival bootlegger gang. If it were the Slippery Rock gang, his party would all be dead by now from bullets. The other two men were dead from a knife wound. A knife wound. Who used knives with such skill these days? A knife was the tool of a low-class thug, not a professional assassin. Whoever killed those men was a professional in every aspect.

It was down to Bo, Robert, and Howard. Bo still led the group and Howard didn't see any reason to argue. If they were attacked in the open, he might try to do things his way, but for now, it made sense to stay together and try to survive. Robert kept muttering under his breath about the crazy lady and Howard wanted to tell him to shut up.

"It's her, I tell you," Robert kept saying. "She's been out here for years. Ever since we found that purse from the city. I know she came with those men and they left her." Robert had the gun loaded and constantly spun it in every direction.

Howard, who was right in front of him stopped. "What did you just say about the purse and 'those men'? He looked Robert directly in the face.

"The ones I saw her with when they drove up here," Robert gasped. He didn't seem to be concentrating on what he said.

"Robert, shut up!" Bo snapped in front of them both. "He doesn't need to hear any of your ghost stories. I'm worried about the human kind after us!" Bo dropped his shotgun and aimed at some movement, but lifted it when she realized the source was a squirrel.

"No, I want to hear what you were trying to tell me," Howard grabbed him by the shoulder. He prayed they were too concerned about survival to wonder why he wanted to know.

"I saw five men and a woman drive up here in a car about ten years ago," Robert told him, his eyes constantly on the trees. "They looked like they were having some party, but she looked scared. Right after that was when we started hearing about the crazy lady. I think she had something to do with them." Robert pulled away and walked behind Bo.

Howard kept his rifle ready, but he hoped it was a human killer he needed to worry about. What Robert told him was too similar to something from his past from ten years ago. Right after the doughboys came home from France. He closed his eyes and tried not to think about Nancy, she would never come back. They never did find a body, but he'd used his connections to make sure the men responsible never would hurt anyone again.

The sky was darkened by the section of the forest. This was a section of old growth where the trees grew together and blotted out the sunshine. Although it wasn't even noon by his pocket watch, Howard was worried they wouldn't make it out by dark to the camp where the bootleggers distilled the alcohol. He was worried about Robert and the way he continued to spin around with his shotgun, ready to shoot at anything. Like the rest of the crew, he was a mountain boy raised on the stories of Nittany lions, although they no longer roamed the hills.

A mountain lion wouldn't use a knife, Howard knew. Bo still walked out in front of both of them as if he was on picket duty back in France. This was a different sort of danger. No gas shells fell from the sky, but they still had to worry about what might kill them.

She almost had him.

Howard fell back from the other two men on the trail. He was tired and wanted to get out of the forest, but they still had miles to walk. There was plenty of mud underfoot, the rain was heavy this fall and he'd spent plenty of time in it. Howard heard a sound of leaves behind him and turned around, expecting to see a squirrel again.

It was a woman. She wasn't that tall. The woman was naked, save for the mud all over her and the leaves that stuck in them. She stood there and looked at Howard for a few seconds before her knife came out. Howard brought up his rifle and she froze. The woman knew what it could do. She stood there in all her glory and resembled something out of a fairy tale.

And then a light of recognition came in her eye. She looked at him and seemed to remember something. Her knife went down and she changed personality before his eyes.

"How-ard," she forced herself to say.

Narla seemed to remember something about this man now that she could see him up close. Her mind couldn't recall much because of the stone that one of her rapists tried to kill her with that day. She tried hard to remember this man and what he once meant to her. There was too much damage in her head to allow Narla to put it all together. Nancy

Adkins turned into Narla of the forest on that day six years ago and there was no going back.

She wanted to remember. She wanted to remember badly. Howard watched as a single tear flow down her face.

The shotgun blast from Bo ended her problems. Howard stood there and watched Nancy go down to the ground.

"I got her," Bo announced. "At least we know who was trying to kill us."

"And who killed David and Buck," Robert agreed. They rushed over to the body.

She died still with the knife in her hand. The three men looked her over and tried to figure out where she'd come from. It wasn't easy to tell under the mud. Finally, Howard pushed the other two aside and scrapped some of the dirt away so they could get a good look at her. The face seemed familiar.

"Lookitthat!" Robert yelled. "She's got a ring on her finger!"

Howard knelt over and slipped it off her hand. It was loose because she still weighed a lot less than she did years ago after living in the forest. The mark on her head was consistent from what the man had confessed to him. The ring he'd given her before she was abducted confirmed it.

"Damn," Bo sighed, "That was one crazy bitch. You have to split the ring with us, Howie. We're all in this together."

"I guess we are," Howard agreed. "Good shot, by the way. I learned to shoot too while I was in the army. Is that where you learned?"

"Hell," Robert said. "We've all been shooting since we were kids. Let's get out of here, no reason to stick around, we plugged the crazy lady and that's all the law will want to know."

"True," Howard told him. "You guys want to know something?" Howard cradled his rifle as he backed up in the woods.

"What?" Bo laughed. "You got something special to tell us? After today I don't need to learn anything new."

"You need to learn this," Howard explained. "I'm with the federal government. You're both under arrest."

The bootleggers went for their guns, but Howard was faster.

As he ripped holes in the drums of hooch and let them drain on the ground, Howard thought about what his official story would be. He'd buried her deep in the woods and she wasn't supposed to still be alive anyway. The other bootleggers might be a problem, but he could always claim a fight broke out over the way the money was split.

He'd done his job and that was all his employers would care about.

Some jobs needed to be finished on your own.

THE SCREAMS OF GHOSTS

ALEXIS RAYE

As she was about to close her email for the night and go to sleep, Sara heard that familiar little beep. A new message was waiting for her. It was an email sent through her YouTube account, which she had filtered as soon as her channel had taken off. It was only 9 months ago that she started uploading videos of her adventures but she had really started ghost hunting years earlier. As a kid, she and her brother would dare each other to go into the creepy abandoned houses on the other side of town. They fascinated her with their old architecture and their decrepit walls. She couldn't believe that houses that looked so lifeless, used to be alive with the sounds of families. Somehow, they never scared her, though she pretended to be for her brother.

She truly loved exploring them. What she loved even more was the attention she got from telling her friends about her brave trips inside. She never had enough of that. From the age of 8 and all the way through high school, she regaled anyone who would listen of dark stories filled with supernatural events that she made up off the cuff. Not everyone believed her but it was hard to deny how good of a story teller she was.

And as a new college graduate from a media arts school, she had dedicated her first year of adulthood into creating this persona of an extreme ghost hunter. Her success was overwhelming, even to her, and her fame seemed to grow exponentially every day. She was now even recognized on the street and asked for autographs. That, of course, made all of her sleepless nights and uncomfortable overnight stays in creepy old houses worth it.

The email was still bold as she clicked on it. It was an invitation to fly across the country to Louisiana sent from "The Conservation Collective of Pre-Civil War Phantasmal Plantations". She read it carefully.

Dear Ms. Sara Elliot,

The Conservation Collective of Pre-Civil War Phantasmal Plantations would like to extend an invitation for you and your crew to spend a night in one of our oldest and most spectral houses. It is called "The Lynch Plantation" named after its original owner, although its name holds appropriately with its history. Mr. Lynch was said to be the cruelest man in the south and lynched all of his slaves when he found out that the war had been won by the north. Surprisingly though, his story is not the one that the locals remember. Called Pi Beta Die by the locals, this house's last use was to house a sorority for the local university. 15 years ago, the maintenance man assigned to the house had a psychotic break and killed all 24 members of the sorority then hung himself on the porch outside.

It is our belief that the Lynch Plantation's history is enough to interest you but to further encourage you to create an episode for this house, we have arranged all of your travel and accommodations. You will see the details in the attached document.

The Conservation Collective of Pre-Civil War Phantasmal Plantations seeks to get more publicity and therefore more funding for our cause so please send your reply as soon as possible.

Best Wishes,

The CCPCWPP

She was hooked. Instead of going to bed as planned, she stayed up all night reading and researching the sordid history of the plantation. It was even more incredible, terrifying and mysterious than they had let on in the email. She knew that a night in this house would solidify her as YouTube's leading Ghost Hunter and may even lead to her getting her own show. She knew her fans well. They would love the creepy historical aspect and eat up the sorority massacre with a spoon. When she was too excited to wait, she dialed the number of her main camera tech Lila.

"Its 6:45am Sara, you better have actually seen a ghost," she grumbled. Lila wasn't a morning person and she had known Sara for long enough to know that most of her "ghost sightings" were fake and in fact was one of the people responsible for how real their "encounters" looked.

"Lila, if you wake up now and listen, I'll buy you Starbucks and give you a raise," Sara said. She knew Lila couldn't resist coffee.

"What is it?" she asked, sighing.

Sara beamed with enthusiasm. She knew that it was coming across through the phone because as she explained the email, Lila became more and more alert and excited.

"This could be huge for us Sara!"

"So you're in?" Sara said, knowing that she didn't even need to ask.

"Duh!"

"Ok ,we have to get the guys to agree too." Sara coached.

"Just promise them an adventure and to keep them when you get your own show," Lila said nonchalantly. Of course the rest of the crew would agree. The guys were in their mid-twenties and could be pacified with a cheeseburger.

The next few days were filled with preparation. Sara responded to the email to agree to the trip and outlined what she needed when they arrive and explained who she was bringing. The impression she got from the responses were that the more the merrier. Finally, they were all on a plane from Washington to Louisiana. The guys slept the whole way, snoring loudly of course. Sara and Lila sat together to write the script for the background and opening. They would shoot the outside of the plantation and house during the day and have shots of Sara explaining all the details she found about the mass lynching and murders.

By time they arrived, Sara and Lila had all of their shots planned and a script all laid out. Even though they were itching to go straight to the old house, The Conservation Collective of Pre-Civil War Phantasmal Plantations contact insisted they check into a hotel and get settled and rested. They would begin their investigation and shooting tomorrow. They were all smiles and splurged on room service and watched TV on the flat screen. The hotel was obviously very old but well-kept and the rooms were modernized for the guests' comfort. The lobby was small but elegant with two rows of white pillars that led out to the street. After they were stuffed, they decided they needed to walk it off by exploring the bustling town around them.

It was a warm October night so they skipped their jackets and made their way down the old fashioned road. The buildings were tall and thin and the antique street lights cast long shadows against them which no one else seemed to notice. The group weaved their way in and out of the busy streets watching the locals as they enjoyed the many bars and cafes. Andrew, one of the sound techs was mesmerized by the voodoo shops he saw and dragged Colin, another camera guy, in with him. He bought them all incense and they laughed as they all wandered the streets with the potent twigs. Finally they settled on a quiet smoky café. Knowing they had to be awake and alert the next day, they all opted for coffee or tea. As they sipped the delicious, hot beverages, they began to discuss the plan for the next day.

"Ok, I think we should be all packed by 11am. I want to make sure we can get to the location and have plenty of time to explore the plantation before sunset. We also need time to shoot the outside shots with the narrative and set up camp inside for the night," Sara said.

"I agree," Lila said. "Colin, I know you have that 4k camera that can work in low light. Hoorah for that. I was thinking we'll start outside and work our way in. We'll shoot like we always do, start in the living room, I'll explain the history of the house then we'll pretend we'll hear something and head upstairs."

"You want me to add a sound effect in post?" Colin asked.

"Yeah, of course," Lila said. "As long as its not too cheesy. I las to sound real. Like a ghost screaming or something."

"I have no idea what that would sound like," Colin laughed.

Lila covered her mouth and made a groaning sound. "Like that."

"Sounds like a bullfrog with indigestion."

Well, you know what I mean. We'll worry about all that later."

"Done deal."

"Of course, we will have to wait until we see it in person to make the final decisions but Sara and I have pretty much memorized the property maps and house floorplans." Lila finished.

"How creepy is it that it's called "Lynch"?" Andrew said.

Matt, their back-end video editor, chewed on some cookies as Andrew glanced his way.

"What? Just cuz I'm black you look at me?" Matt said jokingly. Andrew gave him a little, playful shove and they laughed.

"I'm just saying..." Andrew said with a laugh, "If there is some sort of evil ghost there... you might be the first to go."

Colin nudged Matt, "Don't worry man, I got your back!" Then they all started laughing.

Sara really enjoyed her crew. They were as silly as they were serious and worked as hard as she did. But they also brought her out of her head and gave her time to be sarcastic and have fun. She smiled at them. Then she saw a young woman lean over to Andrew.

"Excuse me... Uh... were you talking about going to the Lynch Plantation?" she asked, looking more than a little concerned.

Andrew grinned, apparently not picking up on her trepidation. "Yep! First thing tomorrow!"

The blood drained from her face. "Why... why would you go there?" she asked, her voice shaking.

"See that girl over there?" Andrew pointed to Sara. The girl nodded and Sara gave a little wave. "Well she is a ghost hunter and also a tiny dictator. We go where she tells us," he said sarcastically. A tone this young woman missed.

She looked directly at Sara. "You need to stay away from there."

Sara laughed nervously. "Oh come on... It's just a house. We will be there one night and that will be it."

The young woman looked even more terrified. "You're staying the night?!" she asked. Her voice carried enough that the rest of the people in the café turned to look at them. The soft music in the background stopped playing.

Sara and her team suddenly were the center of attention. Something that Sara was only comfortable with when it was filmed, not live. She looked at all the faces staring back at her. "Yea... that was part of the contract. My team and I have been paid to make a show for it... to raise money to restore it. It will bring more tourism to this town."

"Restore it?" the young woman asked. "We don't want it restored and we certainly don't want any tourists coming here only to be killed by going in that house."

The other patrons in the place nodded their heads in agreement.

"Listen, I have been all over the United States. I have stayed in over a hundred haunted houses. Nothing violent has ever happened and no one has ever been hurt." Sara said, choosing her words wisely. She wanted to tell them that all of this ghost business was crazy and that she had never encountered anything supernatural, but she didn't want that to get out and damage her show's credibility.

"All due respect... you've never stayed in this house." Another guy said from the corner. Sara's crew looked around at the petrified faces.

"So none of you ever go there? Even out of curiosity?" Colin asked.

"The last person that went there out of curiosity was found hanging from the porch the next day." The young woman replied.

"Maybe he was depressed and chose to off himself there." Andrew suggested while rolling his eyes. If anyone was a skeptic, it was him.

"He was my brother," she said. Andrew looked mortified and wished his tea had a shot of whiskey in it.

"Oops," he muttered, wishing he could say more.

"I'm sorry for your loss but we were paid to do something and we never back out of a contract." Sara said while Andrew stared at the table in front of him. "Now, I think we should be going." She said as they all stood up.

They shuffled out of the café and began walking towards the hotel quietly. They were all silently trying to brush off the many warnings they had just heard and get their excitement back.

"It's ok guys, some places just really buy into this crap." Lila offered.

"Yeah... but we have never had that reaction from any other location," Matt said. "Those folks are serious about this shit."

"Come on guys," Sara said. "This is a beautiful, creepy, historic building. It's going to be great, AND safe." They were probably just hazing the out of towners. I bet they're probably in there right now laughing their asses off at scaring us. Well, we'll let them think that way."

"Hey, uh... excuse me! Wait!" They heard someone say behind them. They turned. It was another young woman who had been listening silently in the café. She ran up to them and stopped. "Sorry, its just... we were wondering... who paid you to come here?"

"Um, it's a group called The Conservation Collective of Pre-Civil War Phantasmal Plantations. I believe they support and restore these kinds of places all over the south and have a lot in this area. I looked them up, their headquarters is just on the other side of town next to a Piggly Wiggly on 2nd street." Sara replied.

The girl looked around at the group with a strange expression. "That part of town has been completely abandoned for 10 years. There was a hurricane that destroyed it and we didn't have enough money to restore it... and as far as I know, there has never been a group by that name in this area. And I have lived her my whole life. I really don't think you should go to the plantation... someone is setting you up."

Sara looked uneasy but Andrew stepped forward.

"Listen, we appreciate your concern but I am sure there is a reasonable explanation. No one would spend this much money on a prank. Now tell all your buddies at the café that we aren't backing down."

Sara looked at the girl. If anyone had spoken to her like that she would have just let them walk straight into a moving car. But this girl stood there with panic on her face. She knew she couldn't say more but still looked like she wanted to stop them somehow. Her facial expression gave Sara goosebumps but before she could even consider breaking the contract, Andrew and Colin started leading her toward the hotel.

"This town is full of crazies." Matt said under his breath.

CHAPTER TWO

Sara didn't sleep well that night. The scene in the café played in her head over and over. She lay awake listening to everyone else snoring. Finally, she flopped over to look at the clock. It was 3:19 am. She groaned quietly. She thought about how excited she had been for this and managed to talk herself back into the adventure before her, deciding that the townies just didn't get out much and had possibly seen too many movies. She fell asleep.

By 11am exactly, their van was packed and any trace of hesitation from the night before was gone and the silliness had returned. Colin was shooting footage of their drive on his phone. Sara and Lila were taking selfies with all of the equipment. Andrew was driving, as always and Matt was snoozing in the front seat.

After a 40 minute drive, passing through the town, driving past the university, they finally pulled up to a large flat expanse. There was a dirt road jetting off to the left and a large sign above it that was covered in dust. Matt jumped out and managed to jump up to wipe the dust away. Sure enough it said "LYNCH". Colin couldn't help it, and he jumped out to take a picture of Matt standing under the sign with both hands flipping him off and a huge grin. They all giggled and rolled their eyes. Then they took off down the dusty dirt road. The large house grew as they neared it.

"I knew it was a mansion but I guess I didn't think it would be this big." Lila said.

"What do you think a sorority was thinking in buying something like this?" Sara asked.

"Simple, they could have keggers and ragers without the neighbors complaining." Colin said. He was the only one who had been a part of Greek life. A part of his past he tried to suppress.

They pulled up to the front of the house and climbed out. For a moment they just stood, appreciating its old fashion beauty and its size. It was gigantic. The wrap around porch alone was bigger than Sara's apartment. Sara and Matt continued to look over the house and the land while Lila, Colin and Andrew unpacked the equipment. When they finished, Lila walked up to Sara to make a game plan.

"It's hard to believe that the townspeople wouldn't want to save this place. It's so beautiful." Sara whispered.

"I know. Like look over there! Past that field it looks like there is a pond and small wooded area. And this tree over here would be great for a giant swing…" Lila said as she approached an old Oak tree that was closest to the house.

"Its really big. Like really big. This is going to be our best shoot yet," Sara said.

"Where should we start?" Lila asked.

Sara looked around thoughtfully. "Ummm… let's begin with the civil war history of the plantation and slaves with the fields in the background. Then I will walk to the tree and end at the porch when I talk about the sorority massacre. Got it?"

Lila nodded once and set up her camera. She began rolling as Sara started to talk.

"Hello, today we are in Louisiana at their best kept secret haunted destination. The Lynch Plantation is over 200 years old and has a most interesting history. Built by a Slave trader and his wife in the early 1800s, this plantation was one of the largest and most profitable in the area. Although aptly named for the fate of over 300 slaves, the Lynch plantation actually received its name from the slave trader who built it. James and Mary Lynch became exceedingly wealthy from the cotton cultivated here. Once the war was won by the north, they knew that their way of life would never be the same. Already know to be a cruel master, James Lynch decided that his final act of rebellion against the north was to kill all of the slaves he held. Most of them were hung from the branches of this oak tree but the younger children and smaller women were drown in the pond at the back of the property.

Then the bodies were collected, placed in a pile and burned at the entrance where you can still see bits of burn marks today. Only 5 years after the mass lynching, Mary Lynch suffered a psychotic break, claiming that the ghosts of those she helped kill were haunting her. She stabbed her husband and then hung herself on the porch right here. But perhaps the most famous suicide on this porch was that of mass murderer Gary Lindale. Gary, a maintenance man from the university was hired specifically to look after the needs of this house while it served as the Pi Theta Kai sorority house. He lived in a small servant house that used to stand just over there but has since been demolished. One night, Lindale snapped, much like Mary Lynch and went on a murdering spree killing every single sorority girl inside. He then called 911, left the phone off the hook and hung himself in the exact same place as Mary.

This house certainly is one of our more chilling explorations and we invite you to join us for a night at the Lynch Plantation." Sara said and stopped. That was the cue for Lila to stop rolling. It never ceased to amaze her that Sara could do these on the first take with no notes in front of her. She was a natural.

"Let's say we explore, take pictures and maybe some landscape footage?" Sara asked Lila and Colin.

Andrew and Matt were right behind, having a heated debate about which sorority girls they thought were the best partiers. Sara and Lila tuned them out, focusing on the expanse in front of them. The sun beat down and even in mid-October, the heat made them sweat. For a moment, Sara imagined what it would have been like to harvest in this heat as a slave. She let herself mourn the loss of the hundreds of innocent lives. She didn't believe in the afterlife so she hoped that death was a welcomed rest for them. They explored until the sun got low in the sky.

"Guys we should go inside and set up now." Matt said, turning to the house. They picked up the equipment from the ground outside and walked up the creaking steps to the front door. Lila pulled out a small camera and filmed Sara as she turned the doorknob and pushed. The door gave way with a small squeak. They slowly made their way inside. The entry way was covered in dust but other than that, it looked as though the owners had just stepped out for a moment. There was furniture set up as if company was expected. The long dining room table was set as though the sorority girls were going to sit down to dinner together. They made their way down the hall and through each room. Colin and Lila were shooting footage of everything. Finally they made their way to the living room. It was beautifully decorated and the fireplace even had logs in it ready to be lit.

"Matt and I will set up the cameras in the rooms and upstairs. Lila, you and Colin make sure that the feeds are working and tell us about positioning." Andrew ordered. He was excited. While the rest were busy with their tasks. Sara decided to watch the footage they had gotten before including her intro. She sat on the dusty old sofa and turned on the camera. The footage was even better than she had hoped and for a moment, she was extremely grateful that she had found such talent in Lila. As the video wrapped up she saw the frame of the entire house. Once more she took in the beauty until she noticed something. She paused the video and zoomed in. Up on the second floor in one of the bedroom windows stood a woman in a very old dress staring directly into the camera.

Sara took in a huge gasp of air and blinked. She looked again and the figure remained. She waved her hand toward Lila.

"What is it Sara?" She asked seeing Sara's horrified face.

"Colin, can you see me? How is this?" They heard from the microphone attached to the camera that Andrew was placing.

Lila moved over and looked at what Sara was pointing at. They replayed that part of the video and they were both speechless. They continued to watch through to the end and that was when they saw something even more startling. As Sara had approached the porch and was explaining Mary's hanging, the woman disappeared from the window and suddenly appeared right behind Sara holding a noose. They both gasped in fear.

"That's good Andrew, I think that's the best shot." Colin said into the walkie talkie.

Sara and Lila looked up to see the screen that Colin was watching. The video feed was of Andrew in the same room that the woman had been in in the video. "Andrew!" They both shrieked. Colin jumped in surprise.

"What?!" Andrew said from right behind them. They jumped and turned to him.

"How... you were just..." Sara stuttered.

"There is a 30 second delay. Geez what's wrong with you two?" He asked. They showed him the video while Colin helped Matt navigate setting up a camera in another room on the second story.

Andrew was just as stunned as they were. "I was just in there and there was nothing weird..." He said trying to talk himself down.

Then Lila got an idea. "Colin play back the footage you have of Andrew setting up the camera." She said.

"What..? Why?" He asked confused. He had been too distracted to hear their conversation.

"Just do it." Sara screeched. He did and they saw the room in night vision. It glowed in a soft green and they saw Andrew fumbling with the equipment.

"How long have you been doing this for now Andrew?" Colin teased but no one laughed.

Then just as Andrew leaned over to place the camera and backed away they saw her. The woman was right behind him holding a noose. Colin, who hadn't heard anything before that jumped back and screamed. "What the F***?!" They watched Andrew leave the room and the woman with the noose remained staring into the camera, unmoving. Then finally she turned her head and seemed to float out of the room.

They sat watching the camera in silence until the walkie talkie beeped, startling all of them.

"Colin, Colin! Is this ok? I don't want to be up here alone any longer. It gives me the creeps!" Matt said.

Colin immediately switched the video feed to Matt's camera only to see a close up of his face.

Sara held her breath. She wondered if the woman would appear in that room too. She grabbed the walkie talkie.

"Matt... uh... can you back up so we can see the room." She said with her voice shaking. They watched for 30 seconds and then saw him nod at the camera and back away. Just as they got a glimpse of the room, the feed cut and they heard a thud.

"Matt!" Sara screamed. They watched the screen and saw that it was flashing between black and night vison. When it stopped flashing, it showed something that drained Sara's blood. It was the woman holding the noose and standing next to a tall man in the same period clothing. And at the bottom of the screen they could see Matt's still body.

Andrew and Colin jumped up and ran to the staircase. Lila and Sara could hear their heavy footsteps above them. Lila stared at the screen with a strange expression on her face.

"Wait... that man... I've... I've seen him before. She reached for her laptop and opened it to a bookmarked page. It was an article from a newspaper covering the massacre of the sorority sisters. There were pictures of all 24 victims and a picture of the man who killed them. It was the same man.

Sara and Lila looked at both images in utter confusion. Then the feed from the room was cut completely and just as suddenly, the power went out. The darkness surrounded them and they screamed. In the corner of the room, a giant clock struck the hour. It was only 10 pm but it felt so much later. After the last chime, the power came back on and everything was quiet. Lila and Sara first checked to make sure the other was ok then looked around them. But when they looked at the walls, both felt as though the wind had been knocked out of them. All of the paintings, pictures and decorations were upside down.

They bolted up and ran to the stairway. As they climbed they saw the upside down portraits smiling sadistically at them. That's when Lila first saw it. Blood splatter on the wall. It looked fresh.

"Andrew! Colin! Matt!!??" She screamed and they ran up the stairs.

"Down here." Andrew's calm voice beckoned them to the last room on the right. Matt was sitting on the floor and Andrew was standing next to him. Colin was fiddling with the camera.

"I just told him what we saw." Andrew explained. "He doesn't believe me." Matt was clutching his head.

"What happened? Did they get you?" Sara asked breathlessly.

"Not you too… listen guys this isn't funny ok? My head hurts from knocking it on that shelf and I am not in the mood for a practical joke." Sara was about to try to reassure him that it was no joke when they heard the door behind them creak.

They turned to see a beautiful blond girl standing in the doorway. Her hair was disheveled and there was blood dripping from the side of her mouth and oozing from her sides and arms. "He's coming. You'd better run… although it never helped any of us." She said as her cold blue eyes looked past them to the window.

Then the lights went out again and flashed back on. She was gone and all that remained was a bloody hand print on the door frame.

"Believe me now?" Andrew said. Sara had no idea how he could care about that at a time like this.

"We need to leave." Sara said rushing to the door. But as she ran into the hall, she saw the same man as before wearing modern clothes and wielding a large knife. She saw blood splatter l lining the walls. He was blocking their way to the stairs. She looked around at the other bedroom doors that were slightly ajar. None of them would protect them. Then she looked up. There was a rope that pulled down a ladder to the attic.

"You guys!" She said as she yanked it. The man at the end of the hall started walking slowly towards her, undeterred by her possible escape. They all scrambled up the ladder and slammed the entry way shut before the man with the knife could reach them. They heard nothing. They sat in the dusty attic and silently tried to think of how to escape from the top floor of a mansion without going back into it. Though they were not really safer than before, the attic gave them a false sense of security and they all tried to breathe. Lila looked over at a box near them. She pulled out a very old painting. Though it was dark, she could make out that it was a couple. She pulled out her phone and used the light to look at the image. When she saw it clearly, she nearly dropped it.

It was the same man and woman they had seen in the video. But not only that, the man was identical to the mass murderer who killed the sorority girls 15 years prior. She read the bottom of the frame, "Mr. and Mrs. Lynch".

"Guys..." She said and showed the picture to the others.

"So what was this guy reincarnated or whatever?" Andrew asked. It was strange to hear that from a skeptic.

Just then, the ladder to the attic began to shake. They all looked around to find a way out. There was a tiny window at the other end of the attic. They ran over and Colin broke the old glass with his foot. Sara slid out first and they lowered her on to a part of the roof over the second story. Then it was Lila's turn. When they were both out, they crawled along the shingles to find a place they could climb down to the ground. They found nothing. By time the guys had slipped out, they had found the only possible way off the roof was to lower down into one of the bedroom windows. Andrew went first to break the window and help grab the others. Lila went first, then Colin. When it was Sara's turn she briefly looked around the property and the dirt road. The moon was much brighter than she thought it was and it lit the whole plantation. That was how she saw him. There standing against an old truck was a man, just watching the house and watching them climbing in. He didn't move.

"Do you see that man?" She asked Matt. He looked to where she was pointing and shivered. Something about the man by the truck gave him a sickening feeling.

"Yea... but we can't worry about him right now. We have to get out of here." Matt said.

He helped her lower down then quickly climbed down himself. They all made their way to the door and into the hall. Just as soon as they had stepped into the hall, the man reappeared with his bloody knife.

"Into the rooms!" Andrew screamed and they split up into each room.

They slammed the doors and turned the latches, each praying that the doors would hold from the phantom killer. But no sooner had they each locked the doors when a chorus of screams sounded. Hearing this, Sara turned around to face the room she was in. There was blood everywhere. The walls were covered and there on the bed was the body of a dead girl who had been stabbed over 10 times. Sara let out a cry. She heard the same sound come from Lila in the room next to her. They were all seeing the crime scenes of the girl that had died in each room.

Tears rolled down Sara's face. She ran to the window to try to open it. She would jump if she had to. A broken leg was better than dying. But it wouldn't budge.

"It won't open. They are nailed shut from the outside. He was very clever." A voice said from behind her. Sara turned to see the dead girl sitting up on her bed, the blood still dripping out of her wounds. He lifeless eyes seemed to look right through Sara. Sara screamed and rammed herself against the window. She would break the glass if she had to.

"You'll never make it. He planned this too well. The others that live here are loyal to him. They will help him to kill you. Just like they did for us." The dead girl said. Blood sprayed out of her mouth as she spoke but she didn't seem to notice. Sara tried not to look at her but felt a pulling sensation and her eyes were drawn back to the blood soaked girl on the bed. As soon as she made eye contact the lights went out again then flashed back on. The room was clean and the girl was gone. Then the door swung open. But the hall was empty. Sara poked her head out just enough to see her crew doing the same. They bolted towards the stairs only to see 24 bloody girls standing at the bottom staring up at them.

"He likes the chase. He likes the chase." They all chanted in a haunting harmony. Then they began climbing the stairs. They turned back to the hallway to see the man with the blade and the woman with the noose.

They moved towards them, slowly at first but then began to speed up, disappearing and reappearing closer and closer. Colin panicked and ran into the closest bedroom and slammed the door. Sara could him them trying to break the window. The woman with the noose smiled as she walked right through the door. There was a crashing sound then a thud. Then the door swung open slowly. Lila ran in to see if Colin had made it but as soon as she peered out the window she let out a horrible scream. She saw Colin swinging below from a noose. She turned back to look at her friends in horror but the door slammed shut once more and both phantoms were gone.

Seconds later there were terrible screams and then a gurgling sound. And once more the door swung open slowly. Lila was on the bed covered in her own blood with stab marks all over her body. Her eyes were looking up to the ceiling as if looking a God.

Sara almost ran into her but Matt grabbed her. He turned to look at the mob of dead sorority girls who stood staring with vacant expressions repeating, "He likes the chase."

"Help us!" He screamed. They ignored him. He grabbed Sara's arm and pulled her into the crowd.

"They aren't going to hurt us. They are his victims." He said and he and Sara ran down the stairs. Andrew couldn't move, he was frozen in fear. Andrew had never believed in the supernatural and couldn't process it. Matt and Sara ran to the front door and flung it open. Sara was about to yell for Andrew but at that very moment they saw a body drop from above the porch and swing in the same spot that Mary Lynch and Gary Lindale had hung themselves year before.

"Andrew!!!" Sara screamed. Matt dragged her to the car and fumbled with the keys. Finally he opened the doors and they both got inside and locked the doors. Sara looked at the house, now able to see it clearly in the moonlight. She saw Andrew's and Colin's bodies hanging from their nooses and looked up to the bedroom where Lila had been murdered. In the window stood the man with the knife. Next to him, stood a lifeless Lila. In all of the other windows, the Sorority sisters stood looking out into the night with their dead stares. Matt revved the engine and turned the van sharply to get back on the dirt road. That's when they saw the man with the truck. He stared at them. His gaze was unwavering. After a few moments he got in his truck and turned on his bright lights. Then he revved his engine and slammed on the accelerator. He was driving right at them.

"What the F*** is he doing?" Matt asked in shock. He didn't have time or room to get out of the way and Sara braced herself for the impact. But as soon as the truck would have touched the front fender, it disappeared. Matt looked around and in the rear view mirror. There was no sign of it.

"Just go!" Sara yelled.

And they did. They drove to the police station and told them everything that had happened. The police refused to go to the house until the morning and Matt and Sara stayed in their cell the rest of the night.

In the morning they all went back. It was just as they had left it. The police did their reports and the coroner was called. When they had gotten all their equipment out, Sara asked if they could leave. One of the cops agreed to take them back to their hotel and they climbed in the back of a car. Sara let her look once more at the big house. She looked up at the room where Lila had died. There in the window was Lila looking back at her. She waved a sad goodbye and disappeared.

Sara was institutionalized a week later and this is the only story she will ever tell.